W9-COT-708

DEMCO

TWEEN SERIES

Kids love reading
Choose Your Own Adventure®!

Watch for these titles coming up in the
Choose Your Own Adventure® series.

Ask your bookseller for books you have missed
or visit us at cyoa.com to learn more.

CHOOSE YOUR OWN ADVENTURE® 9

LOST ON THE AMAZON

BY R. A. MONTGOMERY

ILLUSTRATED BY JASON MILLET
COVER ILLUSTRATED BY MARCO CANNELLA

CHOOSE YOUR OWN ADVENTURE® CLASSICS
A DIVISION OF

CHOOSECO
WAITSFIELD, VERMONT

Illustrated by: Jason Millet
Cover illustrated by: Marco Cannella
Book design: Stacey Boyd, Big Eyedea Visual Design
Chooseco dragon logos designed by: Suzanne Nugent

For information regarding permission, write to:

CHOOSECO

P.O. Box 46
Waitsfield, Vermont 05673
www.cyoa.com

ISBN 10 1-933390-49-2
ISBN 13 978-1-933390-49-9

Published simultaneously in the United States and Canada

Printed in Canada

0 9 8 7 6 5 4

To Anson and Ramsey,
With special thanks to Julius Goodman
For all his editorial and writing help.

And to Shannon, Rebecca, Avery and Lila

BEWARE and WARNING!

This book is different from other books.

You and YOU ALONE are in charge of what happens in this story.

There are dangers, choices, adventures and consequences. YOU must use all of your numerous talents and much of your enormous intelligence. The wrong decision could end in disaster—even death. But, don't despair. At anytime, YOU can go back and make another choice, alter the path of your story, and change its result.

The Amazon River can be misleading. It appears slow and lazy, yet its depth and power have claimed many lives. Has the river taken your friends? Or are they wandering deep into the heart of the jungle darkness that rims its banks?

Beware the strange power of the Amazon River, its many strange residents, and its many myths. Who knows what evil or good lurks around the bend?

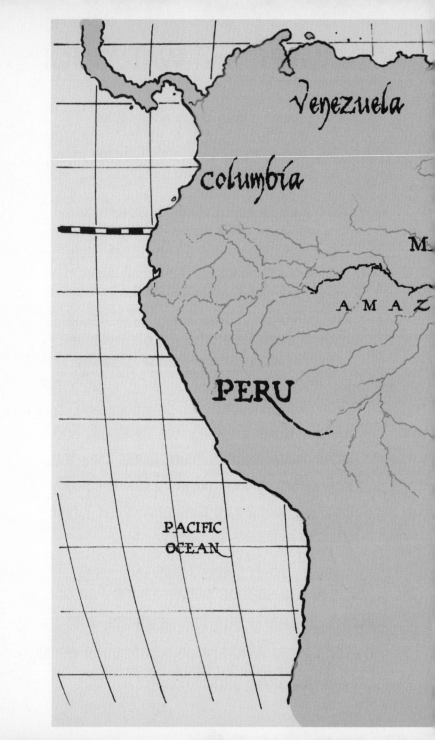

You are a doctor, and your specialty is tropical diseases. After college and medical school you worked in a remote jungle hospital in Africa. There you gained recognition for your work on malaria, blackwater fever, and the dreaded leprosy.

You have stopped at a hotel in Manaus, Brazil, the last major town on the Amazon river. Upstream from here, the river snakes into an almost impenetrable rain forest—dangerous and mysterious. You are the doctor for a small, highly-skilled expedition. Your task is to search for and lend medical skills to the lost villages of the forest people. You will meet tribes of Indians who have never seen modern people and—who knows? Perhaps even the fabled Amazons, women of strength and courage who live without men.

A difficult case at the Hospital for Tropical Diseases delayed your coming to Brazil, but at last you have arrived. You are waiting to be picked up by one of the Indian guides working for your expedition. The others went ahead eleven days ago.

Turn to page 2.

2

You approach the hotel desk and ask once again, "Any emails or faxes for me?"

The man at the desk smothers a yawn and answers in English with a heavy Portuguese accent. "I am very, very sorry, Doctor, but as I have been telling you all day long, there are no, I repeat, no messages for you."

"Okay, thanks. Just let me know if there are any messages. Okay?"

"But of course. But of course. In this part of the world things go slowly."

He turns away from the front desk and sits down to his cup of thick black coffee.

What now? You have been here for a full day. It's almost impossible to get a cell phone signal in this town. No guide, no messages, no clues as to what to do next! It is as if the Amazon has swallowed all trace of your expedition.

Turn to page 4.

You walk out of the three-story wooden framed hotel and cross the street. The sun beats down, reflecting off the road in shimmering waves. The air is heavy, humid, and ripe with the smell of vegetation—a sweet smell that promises both life and death. You wander through the city and eventually end up at the river, where you sit on a bench and gaze at the water, lost in thought.

The Amazon river at this point is broad and swift. You know it is the largest river in the world. The Amazon and its tributaries drain an enormous basin; in all, there are 15,000 miles of navigable riverways. They are surrounded by an expanse of jungle that dwarfs the river system.

On the river you face piranhas, alligators, poisonous snakes, and deadly electric eels, but the jungle hides

more than physical danger. Anything could be hidden here. You stare at the pulsing lifeline of water and feel anxious to join your friends, who have already begun to penetrate its mysteries.

With a start, you realize that you have lost track of time. You must have been looking at the river for hours. You hurry back.

When you return to the hotel, the desk clerk rushes out to meet you.

"Where have you been? Where have you been? We have been looking for you!"

Turn to page 6.

6

The clerk hurries you inside and presents you to a short, powerful-looking Indian. The Indian looks at you with bright, alert eyes.

"My name is Owaduga. I bring bad news. Very bad news. Your friends are lost deep in the Amazon jungle."

You are shocked and don't know what to say.

"Six days ago," Owaduga says calmly, "before the sun rose, there came a song of the jungle flute. It lasted less than a minute. Then it came again and again and again. I warned your friends, but they did not listen; they were under the spell of the music. They disappeared and did not return. I fear for their lives. This is not the first time the jungle flute music has claimed sacrifices."

You stare at this man, imagining the worst. At that moment two police officers, members of the River Patrol, arrive. The hotel clerk has called them with the news of the disappearance of your friends.

Turn to page 8.

"I will go with you, Owaduga."

The Indian looks straight at you with strength and pride. "We must leave at once," he says.

The officers become very excited. One of them grabs you by the arm and says firmly, "Do not go. It is too dangerous. No good will come of it. I will not allow it. You must wait."

You shake him off and turn to Owaduga, saying, "I'm ready. My gear isn't even unpacked. Let's go."

With that, you get your gear, and leave. As you walk out the front door, you hear the clerk say to the officers, "They are fools, those two. The river is dangerous, and so is the jungle. They are lost even before they start!"

Turn to page 9.

8

"This is a serious matter," says one of the officers. "We must organize a rescue party. We will go by River Patrol boat with a force of soldiers. It will take three days to arrange. You must wait here."

The Indian guide shakes his head. "That is not good. We must go at once. I will take you in my dugout canoe. We must go quietly so as not to disturb the spirits of the jungle."

The clerk suggests that you rent a plane and fly to the last known location of the expedition. An overhead fan drones on, scarcely stirring the humid air.

If you decide to go with the guide in his dugout, turn to page 7.

If you decide to rent a plane to speed up the search, turn to page 46.

If you decide to wait for the River Patrol, turn to page 92.

Owaduga helps you with your gear, and soon you are standing at the river's edge beside a slender dugout canoe. The boat is about twenty feet long. An old six-horsepower outboard motor is attached to the stern with a wooden bracket. Two short paddles, a long pole, and a net are in the dugout. Also in the canoe are three spears, their sharp points wrapped in broad green leaves and bound with vines, and a bow with a bark quiver of arrows. Owaduga has a machete on his belt.

"Step into the middle of the canoe," he says. "Otherwise it will tip. Do not move or change positions quickly. Do not drag your hand in the water."

You nod as he gives his instructions, but you certainly don't need them. You are familiar with boats, and you have lived in the jungle. All in all, though, the precautions are wise.

Turn to page 13.

"I can't go any farther today, Owaduga. We must camp here."

In the half-light of early evening you see him nod, but he does not speak. He guides the canoe to a suitable spot on the bank of the river. Together you start a fire. High in the forest you hear the screeching of howler monkeys. You wish it were dawn and you were on your way. There is a strange, uncomfortable feeling to this place.

After dinner, Owaduga makes a hammock out of vines and long strips of bark. The bed looks unstable to you, but the Indian climbs in without a word and goes to sleep. You sit staring at the fire, worrying about your friends, unsure of your next move.

Near midnight you are restless and so wide-awake that you leave the dwindling campfire and walk down to the water's edge.

A splash attracts your attention. Not far from the bank, you see the head of a large animal surrounded by churning water. You bend down for a closer look and slip on the mud. Too late you realize you have fallen into a piranha feeding frenzy.

The End

The woman does not move. There is no sign of fear or hostility on her face. She just stands there patiently. Owaduga sits in the stern, silent and immobile.

You carefully leave the dugout, being sure to hold both sides of the craft as Owaduga suggested.

"Hello. Well, I mean, how are you?"

You turn to Owaduga. "What language does she speak?"

He does not reply. The woman speaks.

"I can speak your language. It is not my wish to speak it; but we have chosen to learn it. What do you want?"

As your eyes grow accustomed to the darkness, you notice three or four other people in the forest shadows. Two carry what appear to be short spears.

"I'm searching for my friends," you say. "They were lost here on the river several days ago."

Turn to page 17.

Owaduga pulls the starter cord. The motor sputters, then catches, and the canoe darts out into the current of the Amazon. You head upstream. Ahead of you is a wall of green broken only by the blue and white of sky and clouds. Quickly disappearing behind you is Manaus. Already the buildings are little more than lumps in the midst of green. In a moment, they are gone.

The sun burns your flesh, insects torment your skin, and the brown water ripples past the bow of your canoe. The day passes. Before you know it, the sun is slipping into the distant green. Darkness will come quickly.

Owaduga, who has remained silent, now speaks.

"Night is soon upon us. If we camp, we lose time. Their trail is growing cold. But the river at night is filled with danger. You must decide."

If you want to continue through the night, turn to page 14.

If you decide to camp for the night, turn to page 11.

You guessed Owaduga wanted to go on, and you were right. Darkness is his natural element. The river to him is a living thing, and he maneuvers his dugout with care and precision. You are lucky to have such a guide.

For hours you travel with just the light of stars and the moon. The motor chugs away.

"Owaduga, could it be the Amazons?"

He is silent, as if he hadn't heard your question. You repeat it.

"Could it be the Amazons who captured my friends?"

He shuts off the motor, and the canoe twists in the current. He aims it toward the shore.

"Be quiet. Very quiet!"

You look into the darkness. Nothing! Nothing moves on the bank. What does he see? What does he hear?

The dugout bumps against a submerged log. You almost jump out of your skin. Then you see it! There on the bank is a tall, muscular figure. It is a woman.

Owaduga speaks. "If you wish, why not ask her for help?"

If you ask these women for help, turn to page 12.

If you don't know what to say to this woman and ask Owaduga to speak for you, turn to page 33.

She nods. "I know. There are no secrets in our forest. Your friends followed the sound of the jungle flute. I fear for them."

"Will you help us?"

"Perhaps. But first come to our village, one day's travel from here. There are sick there. We know you are a doctor. You must help us; then we will help you."

If you decide to continue up the river, promising to come back after you find your friends, turn to page 18.

If you decide to go with this woman, pack up your medical kit and turn to page 19.

SECRET ONLINE ENDING

If you doubt the flute's ability to harm you and want to find out more about it before you decide, go to www.cyoa.com/amazon1510.htm

"I will come back, but now I must go for my friends."

The woman looks at you with great sadness in her eyes.

"I understand. But when you return, my people and I will be gone."

With that, she vanishes into the jungle. It is as if the wall of trees was a magic doorway to another world.

Weeks later—tired, hungry, and frightened, you discover the remains of your friends in an isolated camp miles into the rain forest. Now you must try to make your way back out.

Good luck.

The End

"I will come with you and help your sick, but you must promise to help me find my friends."

"My name is Zagoona. You have my promise."

Owaduga stays in the dugout while you get your medical kit.

"I cannot come with you. They would never let me into their village. These are the Amazons you asked about. You may be the first outsider ever to be taken to one of their villages. Your journey will be a dangerous one."

You wish you hadn't agreed to go, but there are sick people in the village and you are a doctor. You decide to make the best of the situation. You walk away from the dugout.

Zagoona moves quickly away from the river and into the forest. The figures near her wait until you follow, then fall in behind you.

The forest is dense and you stumble over roots, get tangled in vines, and bump into trees. The women move quickly and easily. Every now and then a powerful hand steers you away from an obstacle.

Night sounds penetrate the darkness. Bird calls, the chatter of unknown animals, and the rustle of leaves startle you.

"Be careful! Stop."

Turn to page 22.

Zagoona speaks a few words in her language. The snake loosens its grip and slithers away. You take a deep breath, but inhaling hurts your chest.

"That was a close call! Not many escape an anaconda. How did you make the snake let me go?"

Zagoona won't talk about it.

Zagoona leads on, and you follow as closely as you possibly can. Now and then you see faint movement far ahead, in the direction of the flute music.

"Stop!" Zagoona says. "Wait here! I will go ahead. If I don't return in the time it takes to breathe ten times one hundred breaths, then run, run for your life. Go back to the river. Never turn back."

She disappears into the forest. Minutes later the flute sounds end. You wait, counting your breaths. Your ribs still ache.

Fifty breaths . . . One hundred . . . Then another hundred . . . Finally one thousand breaths.

No Zagoona! The song of the flute begins again.

If you run for your life, turn to page 29.

If you go after Zagoona, following the sound of the flute, turn to page 31.

You sense that these women will help you. Perhaps they are even tracking your friends now. Anyway, a deal is a deal. First her sick, then your friends. Deep into the jungle you plunge.

Dawn comes. Howler monkeys scream, macaws and parrots chatter in the trees, and flies and mosquitoes swarm around you. Spider webs cling to your face. You are drenched in sweat. Still you trudge on. You wish the Amazons would slow their pace, but Zagoona pushes on into the forest.

"Watch out! Watch out!"

An arrow pierces the thick air, thudding into a tree trunk inches away from your head. Zagoona runs to you.

"Are you all right? Did it touch you?"

"I'm fine. It missed me."

You reach for the arrow, but Zagoona slaps your hand away.

"Poison! Do not touch it!"

Up ahead, the other women are chasing the unseen attacker. When they return, they are smiling. The words they say to Zagoona are unintelligible to you. This must be their native tongue. It sounds like no language you have heard.

Zagoona turns to you.

Turn to page 28.

Zagoona speaks with authority. You freeze in your tracks. Your heart is pounding as you peer into the dark, straining to see what danger lies ahead.

There is a crashing sound and a high, piercing whistle. Then silence. In a moment the silence is broken by the haunting sound of a distant flute!

It must be the same flute your friends heard. Zagoona moves beside you and whispers, "Ignore the flute. It will kill you."

"But it will lead me to my friends. That's what they followed." You are ready to go after the flute sound, which seems to have moved farther into the forest. It is strangely alluring to you.

"Listen to me," Zagoona says. "The flute means death. Come with us. Now!"

If you go with them, turn to page 21.

If you follow the sound of the flute, turn to page 26.

In the gloom you recognize the women who were with Zagoona before. They surround you. In their hands are spears. With them is Owaduga.

"Shhh! We will attack when the sun pierces the roof of the world."

It seems to take forever, but at last the time comes and you are surrounded by the cries of the others.

"ZWEE!"

"YARAGUNA!"

Your band dashes from the forest into the clearing. The forest people flee in fear. You free your friends and run back to the river and safety.

Now it is time to go to the village of the Amazons and treat the sick. Then on with your expedition!

The End

"Oh well," you say to yourself as you walk bravely toward the temple entrance. Just before you make the final—and perhaps fatal—step across the threshold, you glance back for what may be your last look at the jungle.

You step into the shadows and move slowly toward the golden light of the inner chamber. Your heart pounds faster and faster.

Then you see them. There are six people, the youngest of them a very small child, lying in hammocks made of the finest mesh. A middle-aged woman speaks.

"Help us. We are dying."

You can immediately tell that they are stricken by the Modatta Strain, a vicious fever that often kills. Your work in Africa included research on this rare illness. But what is an African disease doing here in Brazil?

You set to work using the special treatments you developed at the Hospital for Tropical Diseases.

The drugs work. The fever breaks. Within hours the people are past danger. You inoculate the rest of the village, over one hundred and thirty people, to protect them from the disease.

You are praised by Zagoona and her people. The next day they set out with you on the search for your friends. You feel confident of success.

The End

26

"I must go," you tell Zagoona. "I must. My friends need me."

You leave the women and plunge recklessly into the jungle. Within minutes you are hopelessly lost in the thick forest. The flute music seems to hover all around you.

"I will protect you." It is Zagoona. She stands beside you, her spear at the ready. "You will never make it alone in this forest."

Together the two of you thread your way deeper into the trees, following the sound of the flute.

"What is it, Zagoona? Where is the music coming from?"

She speaks softly. "The legends say the spirits of the forest lure souls with the flute to feed their appetite for human blood. I don't believe them, though. I think it is the Michawa people. They are fierce and angry. We will soon see."

There is a slithering noise behind you. Before you have a chance to see what it is, you are wrapped in the coils of an enormous anaconda. The snake is crushing your ribs. You can barely breathe.

Turn to page 20.

"You were lucky," she says. "That arrow was shot by a Michawa. They come from the region of the Orinoco. Those arrows are dipped in poison— one touch and you are dead. They will try again. Be careful."

For two more hours you navigate the forest until the vegetation begins to thin. You are in a region of low, rolling hills. The rainforest is easier to walk in. Then, as if stepping through a door, you find yourself in a huge clearing. In the center of the clearing stands a large temple made of perfectly shaped mahogany trunks. The entrance to the temple is triangular. Inside shines a bright, golden light.

Around the temple are thatched-roof buildings joined one to another by walkways. This must be the village of the Amazons.

Zagoona points to the temple.

"The sick are in there. You go alone. We will wait."

There isn't a single living thing in sight. The village appears to be a ghost town. Then you hear a flute!

If you enter the temple alone, turn to page 25.

If you refuse, turn to page 32.

Run! Run for it!

The sound of the flute grows louder and louder and louder until it seems to be thunder and earthquake and ocean storm all at once.

You pound through the forest; you race over tree roots; you fly over rocks; you dodge trees. You flee for your life.

Finally you reach the riverbank. Owaduga sits as he did before in the stern of the canoe, waiting.

The noise ends. Only the pounding of your heart can be heard in your ears. Owaduga speaks.

"You have met the Amazons. Their leader has led you from their village and frightened you. That is their message. Leave them alone. They have told me you will find your friends two days upriver from here. They are safe. Let us go, and let them be."

The End

Time is up. You take twenty more breaths for good measure, but still there is no sign of Zagoona. Stealthily you creep forward, following the sound of the flute. You take ten breaths for every step. You move very slowly, but you are afraid for your life.

Finally, two hours later, you come to a clearing in the forest. Birds fill the air with noise.

You peek into the clearing. There you see Zagoona, your friends, and two others bound with vines and gagged with leaves! They are surrounded by a large group of very small people. At first you think they are children, and then you realize that they are forest people.

The leader wears the skin of an anaconda and plays upon a flute made of a long piece of carved wood. He dances about his victims, taunting them with the music, dancing faster and faster and closer and closer.

Then you hear someone breathing right next to you!

Turn to page 24.

You stare at the temple. The sound of the flute echoes in the air. All eyes are riveted on you. You take one step forward.

Then you freeze. There under a thatched roof sit several waterproof backpacks, and the cases carrying their computers and genetic mapping equipment. You turn to move toward them when an arrow tipped with deadly curare poison flies through the air and buries itself in your back. The world spins; then darkness covers all.

The End

"Owaduga, you do the talking. I don't know their language."

You peer into the dark jungle. You feel very vulnerable and unprotected. Your guide talks with the woman on shore for several minutes. Then there is a long pause. She turns to her friends and speaks to them in hushed tones. Then she says something to Owaduga.

"These are Amazons," he says. "You asked about them, here they are. No, they will not help us. No, they do not have your friends; but they know where they are."

Suddenly you realize that the figures on the bank have disappeared.

"Where? Where are they?"

"Who? The Amazons? They are like spirits. They come and go at their own time. No one commands them."

You shake your head. "No, I mean where are my friends. Where did she say they are?"

Owaduga pushes the canoe out into the stream and starts the motor.

"They are prisoners of the Michawa people. They will probably be dead before we get to them."

Turn to page 36.

"I need help! I need your strength!"

The witch doctor turns to you. His eyes flash.

"You? You? What do you want? Why should I help you?"

"My friends are lost. They have been captured by the Michawa. Save them! Please save them!"

The big man frowns.

"Only the spirits can say what has happened to your friends—and what will happen to you!" He raises his spear in a threatening gesture that makes the monkey's eyes gleam.

From a small pouch he removes a pinch of colored powder, loads it into a slender pipe, and inhales deeply. Within seconds he is in a trance.

You wait. Minutes pass. You begin to fidget, and Owaduga calms you.

"Be patient. You will see."

At last the witch doctor opens his eyes. He stares at the sky and speaks.

"Your friends are safe. You will come with me and a war party. We will save them."

The End

Your mouth is dry with fear. You can barely ask, "What can we do, Owaduga?"

He shakes his head. "Trust in the spirits of the forest. If the souls of your friends are good, they will live. If not, well . . ." Owaduga lapses into silence. You can tell he will speak no more.

The dugout pushes ahead and soon reaches a stretch of reddish-gray sand along one bank. Several dugouts are pulled up onto the sand. A fire burns in front of five low-roofed huts. A group of men, women, and children sit before the fire.

Owaduga greets them with a wave, and soon you are sitting with these people. Your guide tells the story, and the people mumble comments in a language beautiful to listen to but impossible for you to understand.

"They say you must wait here until a witch doctor can put a spell on the Michawas. Only then will your friends be safe. There is nothing else to do."

If you wait for the witch doctor, turn to page 40.

If you push on, turn to page 39.

"Mana, Towa, Tona, Guna!
Mana, Towa, Tona, Dowa."

The giant man chants in a deep rumble and the people all bow down before him. His head is wreathed in owl feathers. He is wearing a necklace of alligator teeth. His chest and legs are streaked with red. He carries a large stick with the head of a monkey impaled on the end.

"Mana, Towa, Tona, Guna!

"Who is it that needs my help? Who is it that is brave enough to ask my strength? Who is it that risks death?"

He looks at all the people. His eyes fasten on you.

If you ask him for help, turn to page 34.

If you avert your eyes from his fierce stare,
turn to page 44.

"We can't just sit here and wait! I'm going on. You can do as you like. This witch doctor stuff is nonsense anyway."

Owaduga turns from you and joins the others in talk. You are excluded, alone, cut off from all by language and custom. You return to the canoe and unload your gear. The pile looks fragile on the sand. Reluctantly you shoulder your pack, leaving two small tan bags under a tree on the riverbank. Owaduga does not move. His back is to you. With heavy heart you start off on a path that leads deep into the rainforest.

"Wow, this is crazy," you murmur to yourself. Then you feel it. First it is just like a slight breeze. It strengthens until the leaves and vines begin to move, first slightly, then more and more, until the rainforest is writhing as if in the hands of some giant being. There is no sound. No sound at all.

Turn to page 45.

40

You wait in silence on the bank of the great Amazon. No one talks. The jungle becomes quiet. Dawn finally begins its slow progress against the dark.

When the first rays of the sun streak the eastern sky, there is a rustling in the jungle.

Out of the trees steps an enormous figure.

Turn to page 37.

The trail leading around the base of the mountain looks well traveled. It is free of roots and wide enough for three people to walk abreast. The path seems almost like a prepared roadway.

You walk around the mountain and finally reach the cliffs of smooth gray stone. There at the foot of the cliffs are your friends. They are dead. All of them look peaceful. There are no marks of violence on them. They look as though they are sleeping.

High above, you again hear the melody of the flute. Before you is a shaft of sunlight pointing into a cleft of rock. You enter; there on the wall are carved the names of your friends.

Suddenly, the light in the cave begins to disappear, almost as if the sun is being darkened by an eclipse. Soon it is pitch dark, leaving you wondering: was your own name carved at the bottom of the list? You wait in darkness.

Your name is not there, at least not yet.

The End

The trail to the summit is long and hard. Toward noon it breaks out of vegetation and rises steeply on a rocky surface. Huge rocks form a staircase leading upward. The shape of the rest of the mountain is very regular, almost like steps.

Then it hits you. You are on an enormous pyramid!

You climb slowly, trembling with fear and excitement. The sun reflecting on the blocks of hewn stone almost blinds you.

When you reach the summit, you find a small, flat place to sit. You suddenly realize what the flute was all about. It has summoned you here to the roof of the world.

You sit for days, never needing to eat or drink, gazing over the entire Amazon basin. As you watch, you become aware of the relationships between the flowing water of the rivers and the growth of the plants, the movements of the animals and the shape of the land. You can see the whole basin breathing in oxygen and exhaling carbon dioxide.

As you watch, you realize where your friends are and that they are safe. You know you will see them in seven days. You leave the pyramid, walking with renewed strength.

The End

44

You do not speak but turn your eyes from the man's fierce gaze. He walks through the throng of people and stops directly in front of you. Slowly he reaches out and taps your shoulder with a carved staff festooned with parrot feathers.

"You are a coward. You are the one who needed me. You are on your own now!"

The witch doctor stalks into the jungle. One by one the villagers slip off after him. Owaduga speaks.

"We must leave now. There is a village two days from here. Perhaps they know of your friends. There isn't much hope, but we will try."

The End

A giant tapir crashes through the jungle of vines, dashing headlong among the trees and tangled roots. Swept up in the power of the noiseless wind, you huddle against a large tree.

The world spins as you grasp the tree trunk. A black-and-orange spider the size of a golf ball slides down a filament of web and examines you. Then it climbs back up the strand and vanishes into the trembling leaves.

Silence and calm return to the forest. In the distance, a flute echoes through the trees. You seem to hear colors as well as sound.

You travel on, forgetting your fear and giving in to the music. The colors of the rainforest reveal themselves to you in infinite variety. The trail leads up a ridge, climbing slowly and continuously. You walk for what seems like weeks, occasionally eating some jungle fruits, but never sleeping, always listening and following the flute.

At last you come to the base of a mountain. The sound of the flute disappears, and you notice that the trail divides. One branch goes around the base and seems to lead to the foot of steep cliffs. The other goes up at a sharp angle. The summit is hidden in a sheath of clouds tinged with the red gold of early morning.

If you follow the trail around the base, turn to page 41.

If you go straight up, turn to page 42.

46

You decide to take the plane.

The captain of the River Patrol says, "You are making a big mistake. This is a very dangerous river. Besides, this is a police affair. You should not meddle."

"I am not meddling, Captain," you tell him. "It is my friends who are in danger. Time may be of the essence. And don't forget, I am a doctor. Perhaps my friends need my help. I suggest you follow your plan and head up the river. I will meet you and tell you what I have found out."

The captain agrees to try your plan, and, salut-ing curtly, he leaves to make his arrangements.

Owaduga, the Indian who brought the message, doesn't like your plan, though.

"The spirits of the jungle are not to be trifled with. They do not like planes. Things happen to people who take planes into the jungle," he warns, not saying what kind of things he means. "Please reconsider and come with me in the canoe."

You are firm. "No. I will take the plane. It will take a few hours to accomplish what will take days by canoe."

"Then let me come with you," Owaduga says. "You will need my help."

Turn to page 51.

"I can't wait around here," you say as you rush out of the airport and into a waiting taxi.

Owaduga hurries to keep up with you.

"The Black Kat Café in Manaus," you tell the driver, "and hurry."

The driver takes off down the road. Red dust billows in a giant cloud behind the taxi.

A fretful twenty minutes later you arrive at the cafe. The driver collects his *cruzeiros* with a nod. Briskly you cross the dusty street and enter the cafe.

Turn to page 52.

You rush back to the taxi stand at the hotel and jump into a cab. "Get me to the airport!"

As the cab races down the road, you realize you have forgotten Owaduga. You wonder if you just forgot and left without him, or if he abandoned you.

The attendant at the airport is surprised to see you. He hits his forehead with his hand. "Stupid me! Senhora Portilho was here just after you left, and I forgot to tell her you were looking for her!"

"Well, where is she now?" you ask in a loud, impatient voice.

"She's gone."

"Gone? Gone where?" you demand.

The attendant shrugs his shoulders. "She didn't say. She just left."

That's the last straw! What else can go wrong? You have lost Owaduga and can't go with him, and you don't particularly relish going to the captain of the River Patrol looking like a fool. You come to the conclusion that you have no choice but to wait for Portilho.

Just as you decide this, a short, thin man approaches you. He has a thin mustache and is smoking a black cigarillo.

Turn to the next page.

"Excuse me. I overheard some of your conversation with the slacker attendant here." He glares at the airport attendant, who glares back. "Senhora Portilho is a fine pilot, one of the best, but a bit unreliable, as you have discovered. Allow me to introduce myself. I am Vasco Mendoza. I am a pilot with my own plane. I am a good pilot. Some even say I am as good as the great Senhora Simone Portilho." He glares again at the attendant. "I would be honored if you would consider hiring me for your expedition."

"Thank you for your offer, Senhor Mendoza. Let me consider it for a few moments."

Mendoza bows and retires to a seat across the room. You stand, wondering what to do. You're eager to get started, but something about Mendoza bothers you.

If you decide to wait for Portilho, turn to page 56.

If you decide to hire Mendoza, turn to page 67.

"What about the 'things that happen to people who take planes into the jungle'?" you ask.

Owaduga smiles. "You are taking the plane into the jungle. I am just riding with you."

You like Owaduga. You agree immediately.

At the airport, a bored and sleepy attendant tells you that Simone Portilho, the only pilot with a plane worth having, is not there.

"At this time of day she is usually at the Black Kat Café in Manaus. She is the owner. She will be back here—probably—in two hours."

You groan. You just came from Manaus. If you go back to town, you may miss the pilot. But if you stay at the airport there's no telling when she'll show up, and you are eager to get going.

If you decide to go to the Black Kat Café, turn to page 47.

If you decide to wait at the airport, turn to page 65.

52

The contrast between the clear, bright atmosphere of the street and the close, dank air of the café is startling. You are almost blinded by the darkness and the cigar smoke. Coughing violently, you approach the carved mahogany bar.

"Yes, may I help you?" the bartender asks. "What would you like to drink?"

"I am looking for Simone Portilho, and could I have a glass of water?" you choke out.

The man gives you a glass of water. He wipes the counter, the only clean place in the dirty café, and waits while you drink. When you put down the empty glass, he stops wiping and looks you in the eye.

"May I ask why you are looking for Senhora Portilho?"

You consider telling him to mind his own business, but you change your mind. "I want to hire her and her plane."

"In that case you should be at the airport, not the Black Kat." He leans forward. "This is not a healthy place. You should leave here," he says, and then straightens up. You're not sure if this is a warning, and if he is talking about the café, or Brazil. He continues. "Senhora Portilho is not here. She left for the airport about twenty minutes ago."

Turn to page 59.

"Calm down, Mendoza," you say, but your words have no effect. The knife waves slowly in his hand. It has a hypnotic effect, and you can't tear your eyes away from it. Then Mendoza speaks.

"Nobody wants to go with me." His voice is soft . . . sinister . . . spellbinding. "Me, the best *piloto* in all Brazil. It's not my fault they all died. I did my best . . . the best. Nobody could have done better. That proves it. Just as this proves it." He waves the knife. "Just as I will prove it. You will come with me now."

Dimly you realize you don't want to go with Mendoza. Maybe he is crazy. But if you tell him you're not going, he may stick you with his knife. Perhaps you should humor him and wait for a chance to escape later on the airfield. Maybe you should call for the attendant's help now.

If you decide to call the attendant, turn to page 57.

If you decide to humor Mendoza and pretend to leave with him, go on to page 54.

"Okay, Mendoza, calm down. You're right. You are the best. I've changed my mind. I'll take you up on your offer and go with you."

Mendoza's eyes don't change, but he gives you a slight bow and says, "After you." You have no choice but to walk toward the runway—Mendoza falls into step right behind you. You can feel the point of the knife through your shirt.

Luckily for you, the attendant looks up at the sight of you walking out with Mendoza. He catches a glimpse of the knife as it glints in the sunlight.

As you leave the building, Mendoza grabs your arm. Now you can feel the knifepoint in your side. "I can't get away!" you think.

A shot rings out in the still air. Mendoza spins around, and then falls on the ground—dead. Your arm stings. There is a short, thin line of blood on your left forearm. Mendoza must have nicked you with the knife when he went down.

Your rescuers come running up. With the attendant is a tall woman with raven-dark hair. She is holding an automatic pistol.

"Are you all right?" she says. "I am Portilho. Did Mendoza cut you? That slimy—"

If you say, "I am fine, thanks, and it is a pleasure to meet you at last, Senhora Portilho," turn to page 58.

If you tell her the knife nicked you, turn to page 60.

"I'll wait for Portilho," you say to yourself, not realizing you have also said it aloud.

The attendant hears you and says, "That is very wise. Things can happen in the jungle. It is good to have somebody along who knows."

"What do you mean 'who knows'? And what things happen in the jungle?"

The attendant shrugs his shoulders. "There is a spirit in the jungle and it is wise to have Senhora Portilho along rather than . . . than . . ." The attendant lapses into silence, and with a look at Mendoza, who is calmly smoking, he goes back to his magazine. You can't get another word out of him.

You walk over to Mendoza, who stands as you approach.

"You have made up your mind?" he asks.

"Yes. I am sorry, I will wait for Senhora Portilho. Thank you for your offer, though." Mendoza's eyes darken. He looks like a snake. Before you know it, he has a knife in his hand.

Turn to page 53.

You take a look out of the corner of your eye. The attendant is still buried in his magazine. As loudly as you can, you say, "No, Mendoza! I told you I'm not going! HEL-L-L-P!"

The attendant looks up. He is as surprised as you are to see the knife slip into your heart. Too bad for you!

The End

58

"I am fine, thanks. Senhora Portilho, it is a pleasure to meet you, finally. Especially under these circumstances."

Portilho's eyes glow at the compliment. She nods.

"I have heard that you wish to hire me. Come into the building. We will have some coffee together, and you will tell me your story."

You will never finish your coffee, though. Already the poison from Mendoza's knife blade is working its way into your bloodstream. Before an hour is up, the Amazon will claim another life.

The End

You plop down onto a stool. Portilho must have left the café when you were leaving the airport. Now what do you do? Owaduga, whom you have almost forgotten, begs you to come with him now and forget the airplane. You still believe, however, that a plane is the fastest way to go.

If you go back to the airport, turn to page 48.

If you think you should go with Owaduga now, turn to page 9.

"Just a nick, Senhora Portilho. See?" You're almost ashamed to mention it.

But Portilho grabs your arm, puts her mouth over the cut, and starts to suck. As she spits out blood onto the pavement, she also spits out a single word: "Poison!"

You feel faint, and you're not sure if it is the poison or the thought of the poison that is making you dizzy. Soon Portilho is finished with the job. She says, "You should rest. I haven't gotten it all out, but you'll be okay."

"I think I need to sit down," you stammer. Portilho and the attendant lead you inside and put you in a chair.

"I think you should go back to Manaus," Senhora Portilho says. "Whatever your business, it will keep."

Portilho must have gotten out most of the poison, but you still feel funny.

If you tell Portilho you must go to the jungle immediately, turn to page 112.

If you tell her you must rest, turn to page 64.

The countryside rolls below like green cloth seamed with a strip of brown: the Amazon River. Even though you are not very high—500 feet—the jungle is so thick that you can see nothing but the tops of trees and, here and there, a few small clearings.

Portilho shouts to you over the roar of the engine, "We will make a stop for gas at a small emergency strip about halfway. I have cached supplies there."

You nod and then gaze back out the window. The heat in the plane from the engine and the sun make you drowsy. You awaken to a bumpy landing on Portilho's small dirt strip.

While she fills the fuel tank in both wings, you and Owaduga take a stroll to stretch your legs. Suddenly, Owaduga darts into the jungle.

"Owaduga," you shout. "What's the matter with you?" Perhaps he's decided he doesn't like planes after all. But why didn't he say something?

You feel like running after Owaduga, but you're unsure about leaving Senhora Portilho.

If you chase Owaduga, turn to page 76.

If you go back to the plane and tell Portilho what has happened, turn to page 72.

You leave Mendoza with scarcely a parting word. The attendant at the airport is also the local taxi driver, and for a few *cruzeiros* he deposits you and your baggage at the town quay.

The town and the quay aren't much. A few wooden buildings along one main street leading to the quay—a low pier jutting into the river. Two dugouts with outboards are tied up.

You finally locate the owners of the dugouts. Both of them seem eager to take you upriver, especially after you offer to pay them some money in advance. But when you mention the reason for your trip—the lost expedition and the jungle flute—they become frightened and refuse.

"We are sorry, but we cannot take you," says one. "We have just remembered we are to take a load of chickens downriver in a few days."

"Both of you?"

"Yes. It is regrettable, but there are a lot of chickens."

You inquire after other boats, but can't find any. You have no choice but to wait for the River Patrol.

The End

The hotel clerk helps Portilho put you to bed in your room. A nurse is summoned to watch over you.

For three days and nights you lie rigid in bed while your body fights the poison. You cannot speak, hear, or see, and your dreams are violent.

Then, one morning, everything seems normal. You open your eyes and discover all the members of your expedition gathered around your bed. They're alive! And well!

"What happened?" you ask. Senhora Portilho smiles, and speaks.

"Simple. Very simple. These poor friends of yours were a little disoriented—lost would be unkind to say. I, Senhora Portilho, found them."

The End

You decide you'd better wait at the airport. Portilho has to show up sooner or later; this is where her plane is. Besides, you're tired of the cab. It's hot and dusty.

You're drinking a cup of coffee at the small canteen when a tall woman with long black hair tied in a braid approaches.

"I am Simone Portilho. I understand you require my services."

"Yes, I'd like you to fly me to find an expedition I am supposed to join. It has been lost. I believe my friends are in trouble and may need my help. I am a doctor."

Portilho's eyebrows arch. "It's a good thing you have hired me and not some of the other so-called pilots around here. I will get you there and back out."

Somehow you believe this woman; you are glad you waited for her.

Turn to page 71.

"Senhor Mendoza, I have decided to take you up on your offer." Mendoza flashes a bright white smile.

"You will not be sorry. Let us go. I gather you are in a hurry. Why don't you tell me all about it while I go through my preflight check?" Gathering your duffel and the rest of your kit, you hurry to Mendoza's plane.

Soon you are airborne and flying westward. The Amazon River is a broad brown belt winding through the thick jungle. You wonder how travelers know where they are; the jungle appears featureless, and one bend of the river looks like another.

Turn to page 70.

68

You can't stand the thought of turning back now that you're finally on your way. You want to stay in the town, but you are afraid of getting stuck here.

Reluctantly you climb aboard the plane. Fifteen minutes later the engine dies. Skimming the treetops, Mendoza glides to a graceful crash.

Mendoza is killed instantly by a tree branch coming through the windscreen. You are on your own now, lost somewhere in the dense Amazonian jungle.

The End

The engine noise in the cockpit is loud. Hot air rushes from the ventilators with a whoosh. With the heat from the engine, the plane is stifling.

"Why don't you take a nap?" Mendoza suggests over the roar. You shake your head and continue to stare at the leafy green below.

It doesn't seem as if you have gotten very far before Mendoza circles a dirt landing strip and brings the plane down.

"Why are we stopping?" you ask, impatience creeping into your voice.

"We must gas up. It is cheaper here than at the thieving Manaus airport."

While the attendant at the little strip fills the tanks on the plane, Mendoza carefully looks over the engine.

"What's the matter?" you ask.

"I don't know. Something is wrong. We will fly back to Manaus and check it out."

You can't believe it. At this rate you'll never get into the jungle!

Mendoza tries to help. "There is a small town one kilometer away. You might be able to hire a river guide there."

If you decide to go into the town, turn to page 62.

If you decide to fly back with Mendoza and start over, turn to page 68.

You collect your gear and climb aboard Portilho's old but very capable-looking Cessna. Sliding into the copilot's seat with a nod from Portilho, you watch as she goes through her pre-flight check. You are impressed with her care and thoroughness. She notices you watching her and grins.

"If you don't take care of the little things, they become big things and then . . . who knows what may happen?"

Before she rolls onto the runway, Portilho goes back to make sure Owaduga is belted into his seat.

Then you are off!

Turn to page 61.

You rush back to the plane. Portilho is scrambling down off the starboard wing.

"Owaduga ran off!" you cry. In a rush you tell Portilho everything. She listens without smiling or frowning.

"So. I thought he might," she says. "Tell me, Doctor, what would you have us do? Leave him here or chase after him to who-knows-where?"

Portilho's words bring you up short. Perhaps you should just leave. But Owaduga is the one who brought you the news about your friends. Maybe he knows more.

The heat of the jungle is intense. You wipe your forehead with your bandanna.

If you tell Portilho, "Let's search for Owaduga, at least for a while; he may have more infor-mation about the lost expedition," go on to the next page.

If you tell Portilho, "There's no telling where Owaduga is; we'd better be on our way," turn to page 78.

"All right, Doctor, you're the boss. Wait for a second," Portilho says as she disappears into the plane. Moments later she re-emerges, carrying a small back-pack and two machetes, one of which she hands to you.

"Watch out for snakes hanging from the trees."

When you reach the spot where Owaduga disappeared into the forest, Portilho takes a compass out of her pack and checks the direction. "Okay, let's go."

Owaduga's path is fairly easy to follow. The jungle has sprung back to cover his track, but here and there a telltale broken branch or footprint shows the way.

Senhora Portilho keeps an eye on her compass. After about five minutes she mutters, "I think I know where he's headed. We will take a shortcut."

You wonder how Portilho knows this, but when you ask her, she just says, "I've done some exploring around here."

Turn to the next page.

In a few minutes you break out into a clearing. The canopy of trees above blocks the sky from view. The murky half-light reveals an ancient stone structure buried under green moss and shrubs.

Owaduga stands before a massive stone in the center of the clearing.

"It's a temple!" you exclaim.

Portilho murmurs and says, "Very, very ancient."

"Owaduga. Hey, Owaduga," you say to him, but he doesn't respond. Portilho puts a hand on your arm.

"Let him be. He'll be done in a few minutes."

You sit down on a clump of moss on a large square stone, your mind a jumble of questions. What is this place? What is Owaduga doing? Why does Senhora Portilho know so much about it? You start to question Portilho, but she motions you to be silent, then points in Owaduga's direction.

Turn to page 77.

"Owaduga! Hey, Owaduga! Wait!" you shout as you run after him, but he doesn't stop. It seems as if he runs even faster. Soon he is gone. You stop and listen, but there is no sound of his running. You shout, "Owaduga!" several times. Nothing happens. Everything is quiet at first; then the cries of the jungle birds and monkeys begin.

With a start you realize you are alone in the jungle. You have no idea where you are or where the landing strip is. You turn around slowly. The jungle has closed in on you. You think you see the path you made running to this spot, but you're not sure. You look around again and see three more possible paths.

You take one step forward and are flung into the air. You're hanging upside-down from a tree. You've walked into an animal snare.

How long can you last?

The End

Owaduga has turned around and is standing now, facing you. He looks different: larger, taller, and more confident. He speaks.

"Your friends are not far from here. To help them, you must go on foot—alone—in that direction. You will be met by people who will offer aid." Then he turns and runs away again, vanishing into the thick vegetation.

Senhora Portilho says, "We are nowhere near where your friends were reported missing." She shrugs. "Still, anything is possible in this jungle." She pauses. "It will be dangerous. His information could be wrong. You should also consider continuing with me to your original destination."

If you follow Owaduga's instructions,
turn to page 81.

If you stay with Senhora Portilho, turn to page 111.

Portilho has the plane in the air before you have time for second thoughts. It seems cooler in the plane, with the air from the vents rushing through the cabin, but it is still very hot, and the humidity makes your clothes stick to your body. You feel so damp you wouldn't be surprised to discover fungus growing on you.

At one point you motion for Senhora Portilho to fly lower. You want a closer look at the jungle. She dips down, skimming the treetops. You are so close that you can smell the ripe scent of the jungle.

Your request is your undoing, however. The noise of the plane startles a large bird. It crashes through the windscreen.

Good pilot that she is, Portilho is able to avoid crashing straight down. With a loud noise of tearing metal and breaking branches, you come to rest in a treetop, fifty meters in the air. Both you and Portilho are knocked unconscious.

Turn to the next page.

You awaken—not in the plane, but on a soft bed of moss and leaves. The sound of a flute wafts through an open window.

Thinking this is the same flute that has captured your friends, you sit up so sharply that your head aches and you are forced to lie back down. You feel your head. It is bandaged.

Just then a tall woman walks up to you. She is dressed in a long skirt of snakeskins. Before you have time to ask any questions, she is kneeling at your side.

"Good. You are awake," she says in a musical voice that reminds you of the flute. "You have been unconscious for three days. Your friend, the pilot, is still unconscious. We fear for her life."

"I am a doctor," you try to croak out, but your throat doesn't work very well.

"That you are a doctor, we know. Please do not speak. You need to rest. We also know why you are here. And do not be afraid; we are not the people who have captured your friends. How do we know all this? The jungle tells us. It feeds us, clothes us, nourishes us, and sustains us. You much must rest now. In a while you will be stronger and we will tell you more. Relax now and rest . . . rest . . . rest . . ."

Turn to page 84.

"I've got to follow Owaduga's instructions," you tell Portilho. "I have this feeling that he is right."

"Well, I wish you luck, Doctor. You may be braver than I am. I doubt that I would go alone into the jungle to meet who-knows-what. Here, take my pack and that machete you're carrying; you may need it. The pack contains some medical and emergency supplies."

"Thanks, I appreciate your help," you say as you shoulder the pack and head off in the direction you were told.

Soon the jungle closes around you. You're not sure how you know you're going in the right direction, but you have confidence in Owaduga. The bird cries are loud as you stride off into the jungle.

The End

"Time is short," May continues. "If you want to help your friends, you must act quickly." You feel confused and try to speak, but May stops you. "You must conserve your strength if you are to succeed. I will give you all the information that you need.

"Your friends have been captured by the Cuwatieri tribe. They use their magic flute to lure people into slavery. The jungle spirits forbid us to go near their territory, even though the flute has no effect on us. Your friends must be rescued by midnight, when they are scheduled for sacrifice, another tradition of the Cuwatieri. You must enter the Cuwatieri village, gain possession of the flute, and break it over your knee. The spell will be broken, your friends will be freed, and the Cuwatieri will be powerless."

"How will I do all this?" you ask.

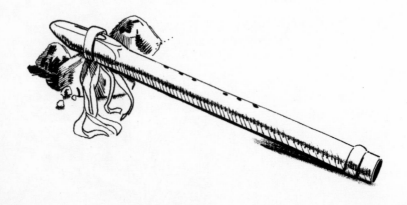

Go on to the next page.

"How you do it is up to you. We can only show you where the village is and offer you this headdress." May claps her hands and another woman appears, carrying a hat shaped like a birdcage, woven loosely of brown vines. It is clearly meant to be tied onto the head with two woven strips that dangle from either side. The cage contains two small green snakes that glare at you with red eyes and flick their tongues.

"Do not worry," May says. "The snakes will not harm you. In fact, they will help you. It is time for you to leave. Will you take the headdress?"

If you decide to take the headdress, let May tie it on your head, and turn to page 87.

If you don't want anything to do with those snakes, refuse the headdress

When you wake, you feel much better. Arranged around you are twelve women. They look almost identical. One speaks, and you realize she is the one who spoke to you before.

"You feel better now?"

"Yes. How is Portilho?"

"Your friend? I am sorry, but she is dead. She died about an hour ago."

"Who are you?"

"My name is May."

"No, I mean who are all of you? Where am I?"

She smiles. "I am May, as I told you. These are my sisters." She points around the circle with her right hand. "January, February, March, April, June, July, August, September, October, November, December. We are the rulers here. We name ourselves after the months.

"You would call us Amazons."

Turn to page 82.

"I won't take the headdress," you say. "I don't like snakes."

"So be it," says May. All the other eleven women echo her words.

Before you know it, you are walking in the direction of the Cuwatieri village. In your hands is a machete; it feels good to have a weapon, but you wonder how you're going to avoid hearing the magic flute and becoming a slave yourself.

You can't. Without your becoming aware of it, the flute has worked its magic on you. The machete slips out of your fingers and thuds on the forest floor. In a trance, you continue to the Cuwatieri village. You are now their slave.

The End

The thought of having snakes in a hat on your head is creepy, but you tell May you'll take the hat. She ties it on your head. It's a good thing you can't see it, or you'd tear it off. May hands you a machete, and you are off, walking toward the Cuwatieri village.

It is dark in the jungle. The moon, even if it were risen, couldn't shine through all the leaves; yet there is enough light for you to see where you're going. You're following a path of some sort. The night noises are different from the day noises of the jungle, sharper and more startling. They seem to have more death in them. You are very frightened.

Suddenly you hear a sound. "Is that a flute?" you think, but then the sound disappears. There is something in your ears, stopping the sound of the magic flute. You reach your free hand up and touch your ear. A snake! The snakes have stuck their heads into your ears to block them!

You panic and try to pull them out but they won't budge. Then you remember May's words: "The snakes will not harm you. In fact, they will help you." You calm down. "So this is what she meant," you think. Boldly you pick up your machete and march down the path.

Turn to page 98.

You decide to stay where you are and keep watch. Maybe everybody is just sleeping, although it doesn't look like it.

You are jumpy and nervous, and every time a monkey screeches or a bird calls, you are startled. Then the light changes. It's almost dusk, and you know that darkness comes quickly in the jungle once the sun goes down. Wait! What's that? Moving through the leaves are several figures.

"Hey! Who are you? Stop right there!" you shout, but there is no response. The figures step out into the clearing. There are twelve of them. They are Indians. All have red designs painted on their skin, and each has a bow and a quiver of arrows.

Turn to page 113.

90

You head toward the circular hut. Your hands growing cold, your back beginning to sweat, you realize you are in the presence of an evil power.

You get closer to this hut, but still you cannot see inside. There is no covering over the windows, but they are black and opaque. You circle once and spot a doorway on the other side. It, too, is dark and mysterious. You approach the door, machete in hand. Thrusting forward with it, you pierce the darkness exactly in the center of the doorway. Instantly the door and all the windows become clear. You can see inside. Floating in the air is a golden flute!

Turn to page 94.

You walk up to the long hut. You still cannot see anybody. "This is too easy," you say to yourself.

When you are within three paces of the door to the hut, you suddenly see six Cuwatieri tribesmen standing by the opening. They blend in with the wall and are practically invisible. Each holds a long spear. You are sure that the spear points are covered with deadly poison and that one nick means death.

The tribesmen step toward you. You swipe left and right with your machete. Soon you stand alone on the dusty ground.

You bend down to look in the doorway. Your friends are inside, bound hand and foot, lined up against the wall. You rush forward, but you have forgotten about the tall hat on your head. With a pop, the snakes come out your ears. The flute! You can hear the flute now! It's coming from the circular hut.

Swiftly you reach for the hat. You must get it on your head, but you're too late. The flute has captured another victim. You, too, are now a Cuwatieri slave.

The End

The captain of the River Patrol grins broadly when you announce that you will wait and go with them.

"You're being very, very smart. You need our protection."

Owaduga is there one moment and gone the next. He simply vanishes. The desk clerk shakes his head and returns to his work. A fly lands on his coffee cup, helping itself to a healthy sip. Arrangements are made for the River Patrol to get in touch with you when all is ready, and then you are alone in Manaus.

Three days later, you are aboard a thirty-five foot, twin-engine patrol boat. Twelve serious looking soldiers sit quietly in their seats in the cabin and the stern section of the craft. They are heavily armed. Two of the soldiers man a machine gun on the foredeck. The hum of the engines almost hypnotizes you as you stand on the small bridge with the captain and his lieutenant.

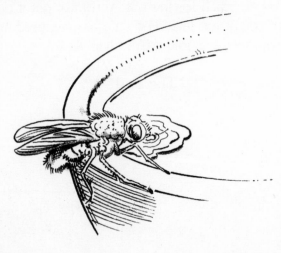

Go on to the next page.

"I suggest that we drop off one squad at the point where your friends were last seen," says the captain. "Then we can proceed up the river for several hours, and leave off another squad. They will move toward each other, like a vise, catching what is in between."

You nod in agreement, but you are more concerned about your friends than with these plans.

"Which group do you wish to join?"

If you decide to get off with the first squad where your friends were last seen, turn to page 101.

If you decide to go on up the river for several hours, turn to page 106.

As you watch, you can see the keyholes on the flute opening and closing by themselves. "There must be sound coming from it, even though I can't hear it," you think.

Without hesitation you rush into the hut. Striking swiftly with your machete, you swipe above and below the flute in one motion. The flute falls toward the ground. You grab it before it hits and quickly break it over your knee. The spell is broken!

There are two small pops as the snakes pull out of your ears. You can hear the jungle noises now: they seem normal. All around you, lying on the ground, where nobody was before, are dead Cuwatieri.

You hurry off to the long hut. You know you will find your friends there and that they will be safe, awakening from what to them will have seemed like a long sleep.

You can't wait to see them.

The End

96

"I don't think I can go another step, Captain."

"All right. We stay here." With a few words the captain has the men setting up camp. One soldier slips into the jungle. A couple of minutes later you hear a machine-gun burst. The soldier returns carrying several dead monkeys, and soon the tantalizing aroma of roasting meat drifts through the camp.

Night comes very suddenly, and you all turn in.

The noises of the jungle are unfamiliar and scary. You can't sleep at first, but at last fatigue wins and you drift off.

You awaken at dawn to the loud peals of a bellbird in a tree overhead. You give a quick look around the camp. Nobody is there!

You jump up. You can see the spots where the other six had their bedrolls, but there's no sign of anybody else having been there. The captain and his men have abandoned you.

You should have gone with Owaduga.

The End

"I would like to continue on, Captain. I'm sure we'll all feel better after a break for dinner."

With a few short sentences, the captain has two of the men hunting for food, two setting up a fire and mess area, and the rest on guard duty. You're too anxious to eat. Soon dinner is over, and you're eager to go on. Nobody shows any signs of energy. In fact, everyone seems to be napping!

"Captain. Oh, Captain," you say as you give him a shake. No response. Everybody is sound asleep. There must have been a drug in the food!

You don't know what to do.

If you decide to stay where you are and hope everybody recovers soon, turn to page 89.

If you decide to go to the rendezvous point where the boat is and get help there, turn to page 104.

If you decide to go on to the village yourself, hoping to find the other half of the patrol or some other help, turn to page 107.

Soon you reach the village. There is no fence around it; there are no guards. The Cuwatieri need none of that. Everyone who approaches is soon in the power of the magic flute.

You wonder where the flute is.

There is a hut in the middle of the village. It is different from all the others. It is circular with many openings all around the perimeter. You can't see inside.

Something else catches your eye. There is a long hut off to the right, beside what looks like a raised altar. Your friends' packs are in a heap outside.

If you decide to investigate the circular building in the middle of the village, turn to page 90.

If you decide to see if your friends are in the long hut, turn to page 91.

"I'll get off with the first party."

"Then you'll be in my group," the captain says. "Lieutenant, take a group of six men to this spot here on the map and have the two soldiers left take the boat to this spot here. If we do not meet in the jungle, we will rendezvous at the boat at 1600 hours tomorrow."

"Yes, Captain."

You are now at your drop point. The soldiers ease the boat near a shallow spot, and you all splash off and climb onto the bank. Without a nod or a wave, the captain leads you into the jungle.

The sound and smell of the river quickly fade and are replaced by a lush, rotten smell of vegetation and the screeches of birds and monkeys. The soldier in the lead hacks through the vegetation with his machete. You are glad you are near the end of the line; the soldiers in front constantly pluck spider webs from their faces.

Turn to the next page.

102

You march for hours. It is impossible to tell the time from the sun because of the canopy of trees overhead. You cannot see even rays of sunlight, much less the sun itself.

The captain calls a halt. "We will stop to eat now," he says. "We are several hours away from the village where your friends disappeared. There is a trail that we can follow from this clearing. But the jungle is dangerous at night. I would like to stay the night here and leave in the early morning. But, if you wish, we will continue on after eating."

If you decide you're too tired to continue and you'll stop for the night, turn to page 96.

If you decide to continue after some dinner, turn to page 97.

A rocket hits the patrol boat.

In a flash of red and white and brilliant orange, you depart this Earth.

The End

You decide you've got to get help from the boat. There's no telling what you'll find at the village, and something is obviously very wrong here.

You don't make it very far, though. Along the way

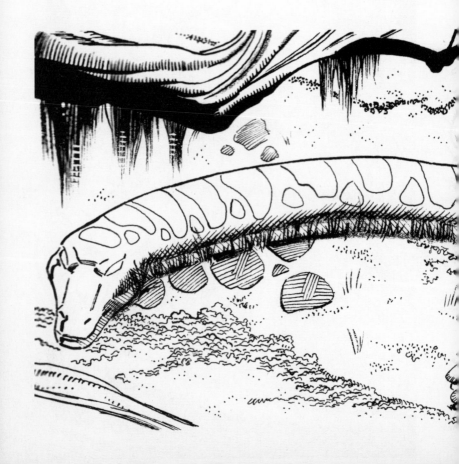

you run into a large, hungry anaconda. The Indians of the jungle say the anaconda is the Spirit of the Amazon and that anyone swallowed by the snake lives, unharmed, inside forever. If that's true, send a postcard.

The End

You stay aboard while a squad of six men and the lieutenant disembark. The clank of weapons and equipment is loud, but the noise is quickly swallowed by the dense rainforest.

"*Adios*, Lieutenant. May you have good luck and a long life." The captain waves to his men, and in minutes they have disappeared into the rainforest. Your boat now moves farther up the Amazon, confronting a bewildering series of twists and turns as tributary streams join the mighty river. The captain seems confident, but you aren't sure he really knows what he is doing.

"How can anyone know this maze of streams, islands, and channels?" you ask the captain, but he's too busy looking at the riverbank.

"This is it!" the captain says. "I can tell it is the right place. We will put in here." The patrol boat reverses its engines and backs against the current. Then it moves forward until it enters a narrow stream. Slowly and carefully the boat nudges upstream.

One of the soldiers moves away from the machine gun. As he stands up, a low branch catches him and spins him into the water.

Turn to page 109.

You decide to head toward the village. Maybe you will meet the other patrol there.

The trail from the clearing is easy to follow, but it is narrow and you have to watch your step so you don't trip over roots.

The longer you walk, the less wildlife you see and hear. While you are puzzling about that, you step into a large clearing. The village! Sitting in the clearing, surrounded by circular huts, is a large man on a throne. He is facing you. He has on a tall white headdress and a robe made of white feathers. Behind him are three ranks of warriors with spears. Arranged on either side of him are your friends!

"Welcome," says the man on the throne. "We have been expecting you."

Turn to page 110.

"YAI-EEE!"

There is a swirling, frothing wildness in the water as hundreds of piranhas make short work of the soldier. You stare at the spot in disbelief.

A roaring blast rips through the air. A rocket explodes in a geyser of water next to the boat.

"*Banditos, banditos*! Fire!"

The soldiers open up with their weapons, shooting blindly into the rainforest.

Zabroom! Swoosh, zabroom!

Two more rockets hurtle through the air. One explodes on the foredeck, knocking the soldiers and the machine gun into the water.

What should you do? Run for it, get off this boat right now? Or should you stay with the remaining soldiers? The captain is nowhere to be seen.

If you run for it, turn to page 114.

If you stay, turn to page 103.

110

"Expecting me? What do you mean? What is going on here?"

Then you notice that everyone is smiling, even your friends.

As you hug them in greeting and they hug you, the villagers dance around you, shouting their approval.

"Two days ago," your friend Chris says, "We were rescued from the magic grip of the flute music by a mysterious group of warrior natives—all women. Owaduga, who was sent by the chief to get you, returned without you, reporting that you were coming with the River Patrol."

"The River Patrol!" you gasp. "They need help!"

The chief sends out a rescue party. They will be safe by nightfall.

You begin helping with the preparations for a huge feast in the village.

The End

"I think I should continue with you," you tell Portilho. She shrugs.

"If that is your decision, let us go." She turns, and slips out of the clearing into the jungle. You follow.

Portilho moves easily through the thick vegetation, but you find it tough going. Vines get tangled around your body, and your hands soon are raw from pushing away the vegetation.

The intense heat of the jungle forces you to stop. You slump against a tree. Senhora Portilho, who hasn't seen you stop, continues. In a moment you feel better and put your hand out to push yourself up. Instead of tree trunk, however, you brush against a small green tree frog. The slime it leaves on your hand startles you, but you soon recover from your fright.

You won't recover, though, from the poison in the slime. Even now it is working its way through your blood.

The End

"Senhora Portilho, I have urgent business that will not keep. My friends . . ."

"Yes, I know. It is the rumor in all Manaus about your expedition. Come with me. We will find your friends and rescue them—if they are still alive."

You think it must be the fading effects of the poison that send chills up and down your spine at Portilho's words. You feel strange, but you are full of hope as you follow the pilot out to her plane.

The End

The Indians ignore you. Silently they pick up the captain and his men and carry them into the jungle. You run up to one and stop him. Your hand goes right through his shoulder! They're ghosts! Even your machete has no effect.

With your mouth wide open, you watch the others disappear into the jungle. Then another Indian—or is it one of the group?—appears in the clearing. His bow is drawn. Before you can move, he speaks.

"We've had enough of your meddling. Leave us alone. Go back to your own place."

The End

"I'm out of here!" With that you leap from the patrol boat, which is now on fire, and head into the rainforest. Within minutes you are lost in the thick vegetation. The sound of firing continues, but now it seems like a harmless popping, not the vicious snarl of bullets meant for killing.

Large mosquitoes swarm around your head and arms, and smaller biting bugs creep under your collar and around your ankles. You stop to rest and fall asleep.

When you waken, you are surrounded by women. They wear clothes of brilliant colors, and they carry beautifully made bows and quivers of arrows. One of them moves close to you and speaks.

"Do not be afraid; we are friendly. You will be safe with us. Oh, and do not worry about your friends. They are waiting for you back at the village."

"What about the River Patrol?"

"The soldiers and the *banditos* deserve each other. Let them be."

The End

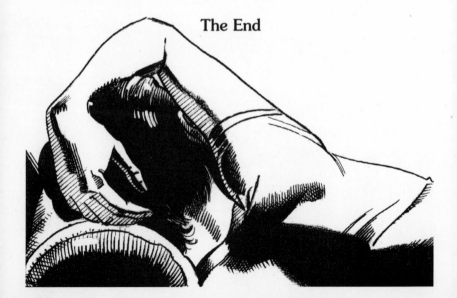

GLOSSARY

Amazon River Basin – The Amazon River is the world's largest river and second in length only to the Nile. With more than 1,000 tributaries, it is no wonder the Amazon River and its Basin, covering one third of South America, are so special. The "basin" or area drained by this mighty river is a hugely important ecosystem containing the world's largest tropical rain forest. The rain forest is home to thousands of species of plants, animals, and birds. More than 2,000 different kinds of fish live in the Amazon River alone. This type of natural diversity is what makes the Amazon so important to our planet. Many medicines, foods and other products have been discovered because of the plants and animals in the rain forest. Development and burning of this area is causing the extinction of many species, some not yet even named or studied by man.

Anaconda – A huge, green snake found in South America that kills prey by coiling itself around the victim. Anacondas suffocate their prey by literally squeezing the life out of them. These powerful snakes can grow to 30 ft. (9.1 meters) and love the water. Anacondas, while deadly, are not venomous. Their ability to crush bones and suffocate living creatures is what makes them so feared.

Cessna – The Cessna company specializes in small planes, usually with two engines, that can land without a long runway. For more than 75 years, Cessnas have allowed humans to safely visit remote parts of the world. These airplanes are used in the Amazon region and other undeveloped areas where landing strips are little more than dirt roads or small clearings in the jungle.

Cruzeiro – A *cruzeiro real* is the currency unit of Brazil. Internationally, it is more commonly called a *real* (ray-al). A *cruzeiro real* contains 1,000 *cruzeiros,* the previous currency.

Howler monkey – A type of monkey who lives in the tropical rain forest canopy in Central and South America. "Howlers" get their name from the startling and loud crying sound they make. Their eerie cries can be heard from nearly three miles away! Howlers are black or brown, have a five-toe grasp and often hang upside down by their strong tails.

Macaw - A type of colorful and noisy parrot that lives in Central or South America. Macaws have brilliantly colored feathers, tails as long as their bodies and powerful, curved beaks. They are extremely intelligent and are fond of humans. Macaws are declining in the wild because too many have been captured for pets and due to the loss of their rainforest habitat.

Machete – A large, extremely sharp knife that is heavy and carried by many rural South Americans. Machetes can be deadly weapons. More often, they are used in a back and forth slashing motion to cut a path through the rain forest. Local guides consider machetes essential for travel in the rain forest.

Manaus – A Brazilian city located where the Rio Negro tributary flows into the Amazon River. It was founded in the 1660s and was known as the center for trading wild rubber. Today, Manaus has a population of just over 1,000,000 people and is the business center for the upper Amazon region.

Piranha – A small carnivorous fish found in freshwater in South America. "Carnivorous" means they eat meat. These deadly fish will attack an animal or even a human in the water if they smell blood. An entire school of piranhas can eat all the flesh off an animal in a matter of minutes.

Preflight – A series of tests done by a pilot before taking a plane off the ground. Preflights include a standard checklist of mechanical items as well as things like checking the plane's fuel level. They are done before every flight to make sure the airplane is safe. Preflights can make the difference between a safe flight and a disaster.

Tapir – A jungle animal related to horses and rhinos. Tapirs are primarily nocturnal and love water. They even go underwater to walk on the bottom of rivers or ponds. These mammals will eat almost anything, but a favorite food is the banana. Unfortunately, all four species of tapirs are now in danger of extinction because of the burning of rainforests and increased development in and near the jungle.

Tributary – A small river or stream that flows into a larger body of water. For instance, a large river like the Amazon has more than 1,000 tributaries or bodies of water that "contribute" or give their water to this huge river.

CREDITS

Illustrator: Jason Millet. Since graduating from Chicago's American Academy of Art, Jason Millet has created artwork for companies ranging from Disney® to Absolut®. His client list includes Warner Brothers®, Major League Baseball®, the Chicago Bulls® and Hallmark®, among many others.

Cover Artist: Marco Cannella was born in Ascoli Piceno, Italy on September 29, 1972. Marco started his career in art as decorator and illustrator when he was a college student. He became a full-time professional in 2001 when he received the flag-prize for the "Palio della Quintana" (one of the most important Italian historical games). Since then, he has worked as illustrator for the Studio Inventario in Bologna. He has also worked as scenery designer for professional theater companies. He works for the production company ASP srl in Rome as character designer and set designer on the preproduction of a CG feature film. In 2004 he moved to Banglore, India to work full-time on this project as art director.

This book was brought to life by a great group of people:

Shannon Gilligan, Publisher
Gordon Troy, General Counsel
Jason Gellar, Sales Director
Melissa Bounty, Senior Editor
Stacey Boyd, Designer

Thanks to everyone involved!

Buy the paperback version of this title and others a www.cyoa.com.

ABOUT THE AUTHOR

R. A. MONTGOMERY has hiked in the Himalayas, climbed mountains in Europe, scuba-dived in Central America, and worked in Africa. He lives in France in the winter, travels frequently to Asia, and calls Vermont home. Montgomery graduated from Williams College and attended graduate school at Yale University and NYU. His interests include macroeconomics, geo-politics, mythology, history, mystery novels, and music. He has two grown sons, a daughter-in-law, and two granddaughters. His wife, Shannon Gilligan, is an author and noted interactive game designer. Montgomery feels that the new generation of people under 15 is the most important asset in our world.

**For games, activities and other fun stuff,
or to write to R. A. Montgomery,
visit us online at CYOA.com**